Hello! Good-bye!

ALIKI

GREENWILLOW BOOKS, NEW YORK

Watercolor paints, colored pencils, and a
black pen were used for the full-color art.
The text type is Souvenir.

Printed in Singapore by Tien Wah Press
First Edition 10 9 8 7 6 5 4 3 2 1

Library of Congress Cataloging-in-Publication Data
Hello! Good-bye! / by Aliki.
p.   cm.
Summary: Describes some of the many ways, both verbal
and nonverbal, that people say hello and good-bye.
ISBN 0-688-14333-4 (trade).   ISBN 0-688-14334-2 (lib. bdg.)
1. Salutations—Juvenile literature.   2. Farewells—Juvenile literature.
3. Interpersonal communication.]   I. Title.   GT3050.A43
1996   395—dc20   95-25090   CIP   AC

HELLO is a welcome.

Sometimes it is a spectacular welcome.

HELLO is a greeting that can be said in other words.

for Pauline and Angela Manos

HELLO. GOOD-BYE.

Every day we use these words.
In one way or another we say them
again and again.
We say "hello" when we meet.
We say "good-bye" when we part.
They are a beginning and an end.

Life begins with a HELLO.

HELLO is an introduction.

HELLO can be said with no words.

wave	shake	hug
kiss	bow	curtsy
sign	slap	tip

Sometimes—without words—a HELLO looks like a GOOD-BYE.

In some languages HELLO has another meaning.

In Hebrew we say "Peace."

In Greek we say "Your health."

In Hawaiian we say "Love."

In Hindi we say "I greet you."

A HELLO can be an ovation.

A HELLO can be a salute.

In a letter the "hello" is called the salutation.

A fanfare is a musical HELLO.

HELLO comes in assorted moods.

funny

playful

friendly   dreaded

expectant   wary

A HELLO can be so *loud* it makes an echo

or as *quiet* as a mouse.

A HELLO can be unexpected

or embarrassing

or just plain wonderful.

At an airport people are always saying HELLO

and GOOD-BYE.

HELLOS seem happier and GOOD-BYES seem sadder
when families and friends live far apart.

There are GOOD-BYES for travelers.

There are GOOD-BYES in other languages.

*Sometimes the same word is used to say HELLO.

There are other words that mean GOOD-BYE.

A GOOD-BYE can be for a short time

or a long time.

But *not* saying GOOD-BYE is always rude.

Some GOOD-BYES are easy to say.

Some GOOD-BYES are hard to say.

A GOOD-BYE that lasts forever hurts the most.

The best time for a GOOD-BYE is when the sun goes down

and the moon comes up.